LEWIS CARDINAL'S FIRST WINTER

Written by
Amy Crane Johnson

Illustrated by
Robb Mommaerts

For Aunt Mickey, who loves the cardinals
– Amy

To my grandma and grandpa, who have always been so supportive of me
– Robb

Johnson, Amy Crane.

Lewis Cardinal's First Winter : a Solomon Raven story / written by Amy Crane Johnson;
illustrated by Robb Mommaerts. —McHenry, IL : Raven Tree Press, 2009.

p. ; cm.

SUMMARY: Lewis Cardinal is confused as his woodland friends get ready for winter. Should he stay or go?
Solomon Raven explains hibernation and migration, leading Lewis to understand the process
of change and friendship. Winter theme of the Solomon Raven series.

English–Only Edition
ISBN: 978-1-934960-60-8 Hardcover
ISBN: 978-1-934960-61-5 Paperback

Bilingual Edition
ISBN: 978-0-9724973-5-0 Hardcover

Audience: ages 4-8
Title available in English-only or bilingual English-Spanish editions

1. Friendship--Juvenile fiction. 2. Cardinals (Birds)--Juvenile fiction. 3. Winter--Juvenile fiction.
4. Birds--Migration--Juvenile fiction. 5. Hibernation--Juvenile fiction. [1. Friendship--Fiction.
2. Cardinals (Birds)--Fiction. 3. Birds-- Migration--Fiction. 4. Winter--Fiction. 5. Hibernation--Fiction.]
I. Mommaerts, Robb . II. Title. III. Series.

Library of Congress Control Number: 2009921096

Printed in Taiwan
10 9 8 7 6 5 4 3 2 1
First Edition

Free activities for this book are available at www.raventreepress.com.

LEWIS CARDINAL'S FIRST WINTER

Written by
Amy Crane Johnson

Illustrated by
Robb Mommaerts

Raven Tree Press
A Division of Delta Systems Co., Inc.
www.raventreepress.com

Lewis Cardinal sat on the lowest branch of his hickory tree.

He was sad. This was his first winter in the north woods.

He was sure he should be busy like everyone else.

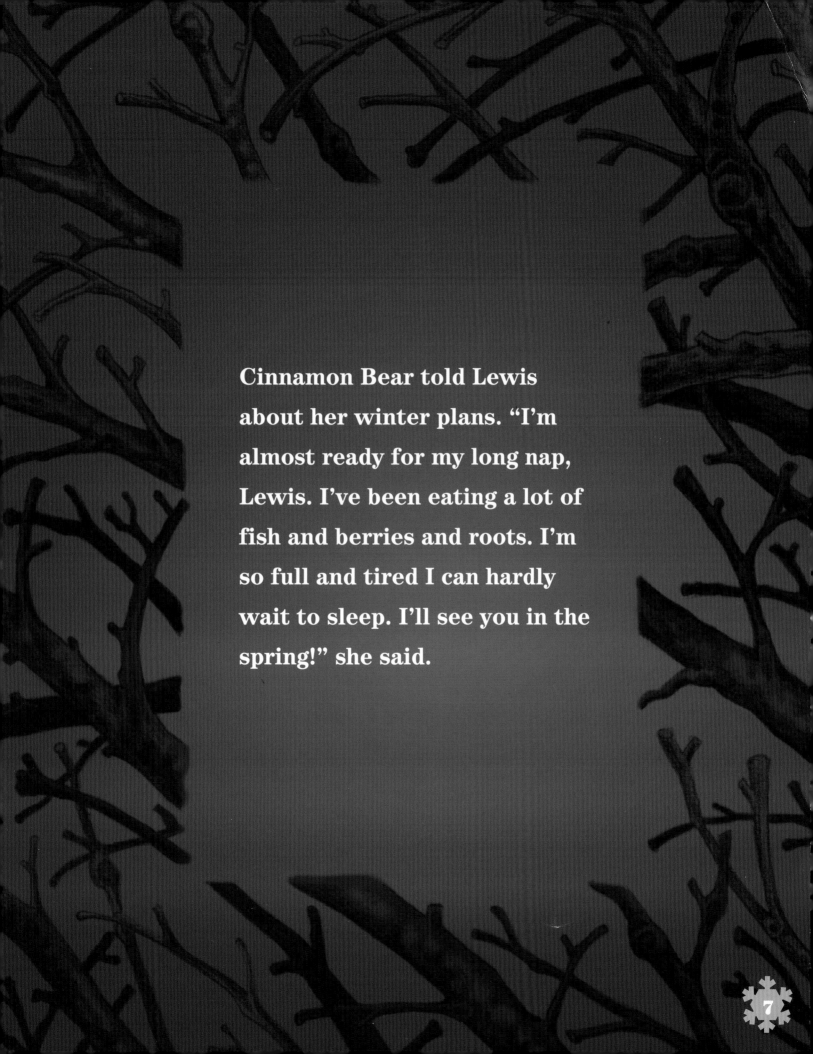

Cinnamon Bear told Lewis about her winter plans. "I'm almost ready for my long nap, Lewis. I've been eating a lot of fish and berries and roots. I'm so full and tired I can hardly wait to sleep. I'll see you in the spring!" she said.

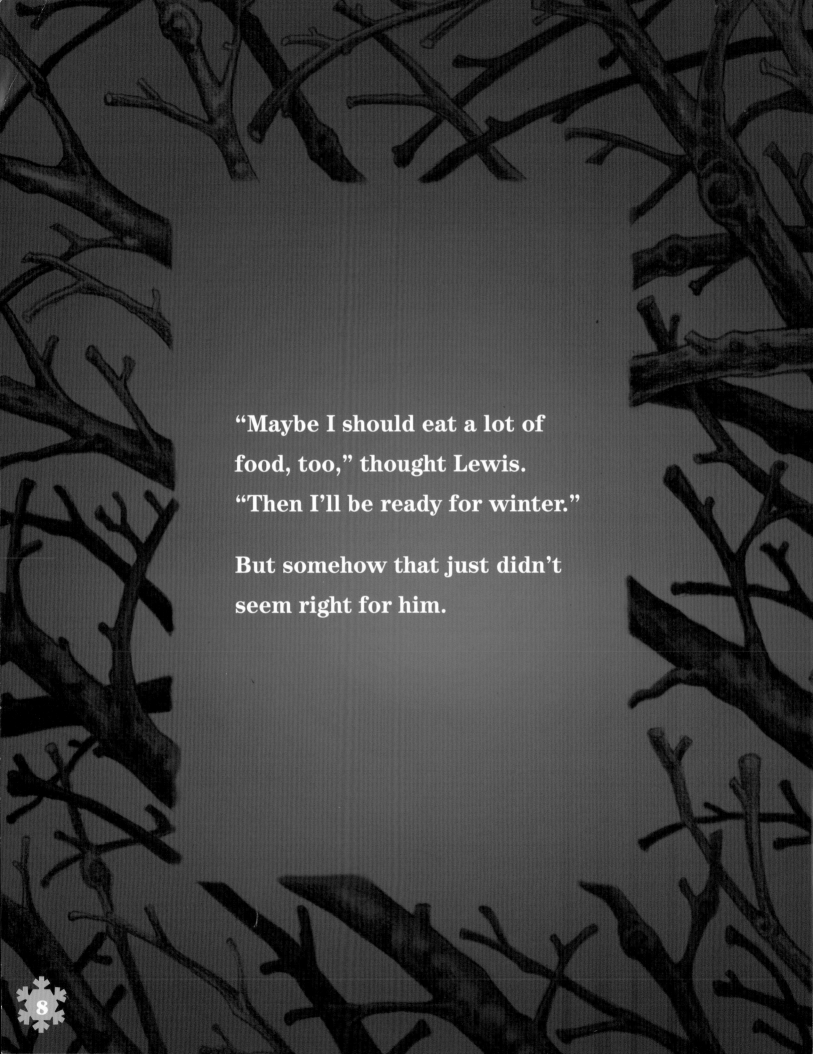

"Maybe I should eat a lot of
food, too," thought Lewis.
"Then I'll be ready for winter."

But somehow that just didn't
seem right for him.

Lewis flew off to see how the other animals were getting ready for winter. He swooped down to the creek, where Polly was busy burying herself in mud and leaves.

"I'm okay, Lewis. This is the way some frogs get ready for winter," she said.

Lewis didn't think Polly's way would work for him.

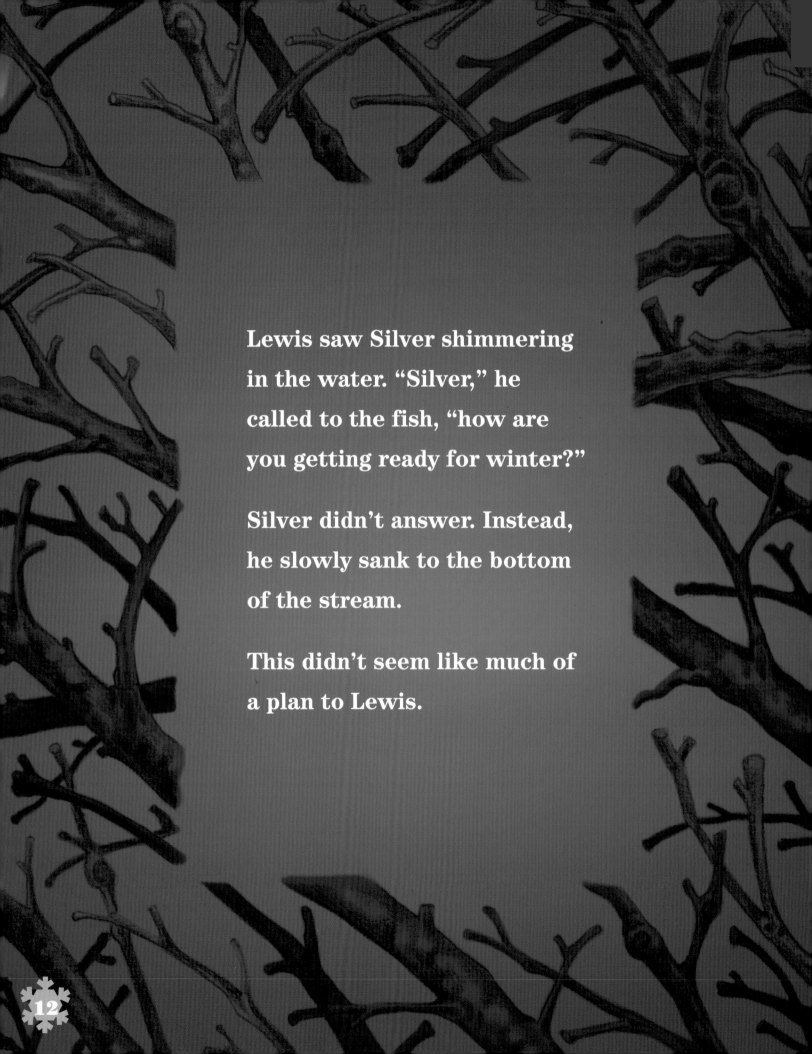

Lewis saw Silver shimmering in the water. "Silver," he called to the fish, "how are you getting ready for winter?"

Silver didn't answer. Instead, he slowly sank to the bottom of the stream.

This didn't seem like much of a plan to Lewis.

13

Back at the hickory tree, Roberta and her robin friends chirped farewell. "So long, Lewis. We'll be back soon!"

"How soon is soon?" Lewis asked, but it was too late. They were already gone.

Lewis moaned. "I'm a bird too. I'm sure I should be doing something or going somewhere for the winter."

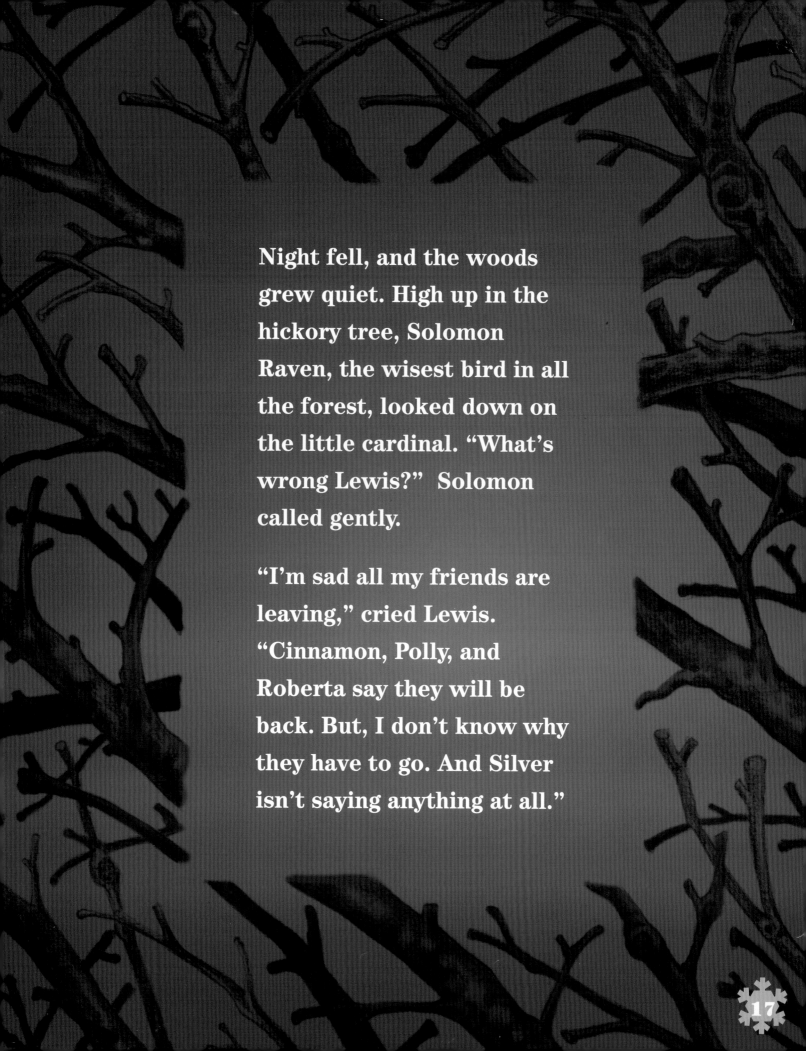

Night fell, and the woods grew quiet. High up in the hickory tree, Solomon Raven, the wisest bird in all the forest, looked down on the little cardinal. "What's wrong Lewis?" Solomon called gently.

"I'm sad all my friends are leaving," cried Lewis. "Cinnamon, Polly, and Roberta say they will be back. But, I don't know why they have to go. And Silver isn't saying anything at all."

"Well, Cinnamon and Polly hibernate, like all bears and frogs," explained Solomon. "That means they sleep part or most of the winter when it would be hard to find food. Roberta Robin migrates each year. She flies away to a warm place, but she always comes back. And Silver stays right in the stream. You'll see, Lewis. It will be all right."

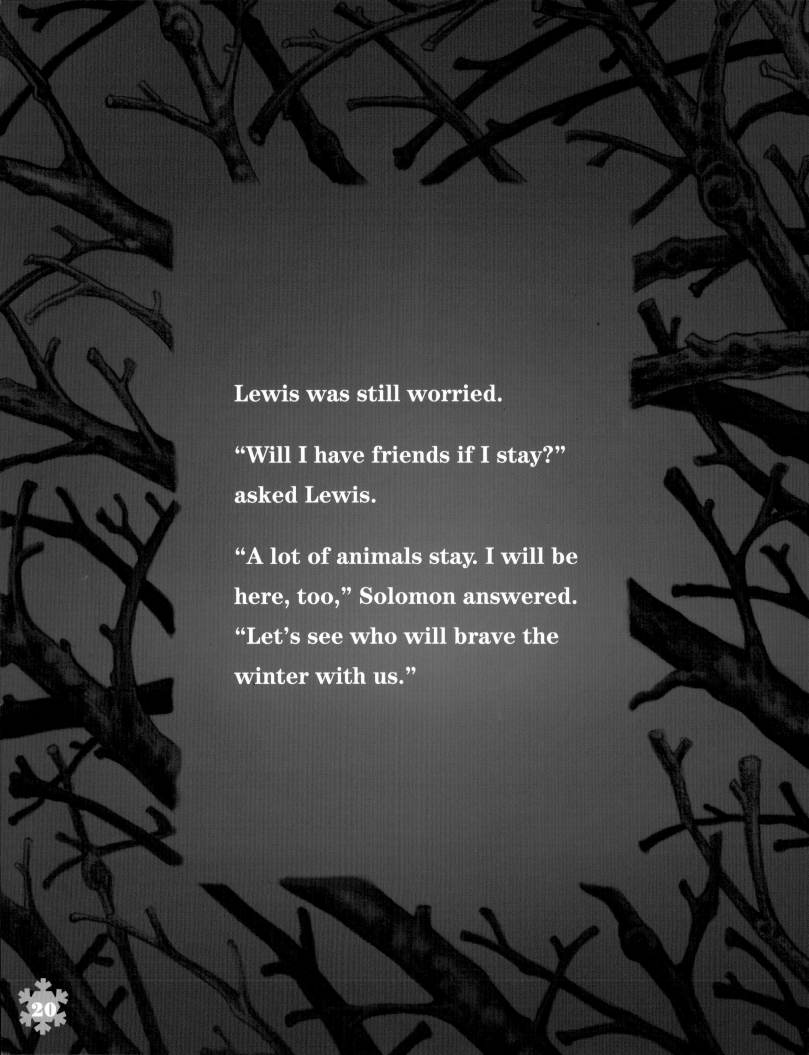

Lewis was still worried.

"Will I have friends if I stay?" asked Lewis.

"A lot of animals stay. I will be here, too," Solomon answered. "Let's see who will brave the winter with us."

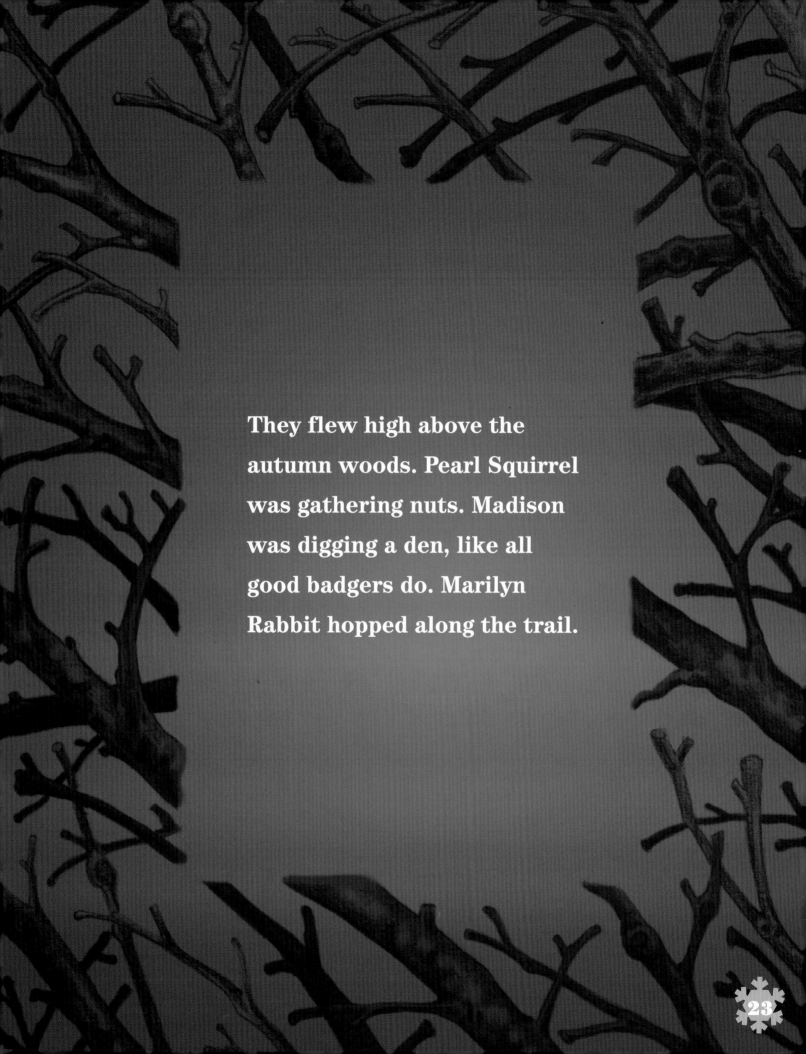

They flew high above the autumn woods. Pearl Squirrel was gathering nuts. Madison was digging a den, like all good badgers do. Marilyn Rabbit hopped along the trail.

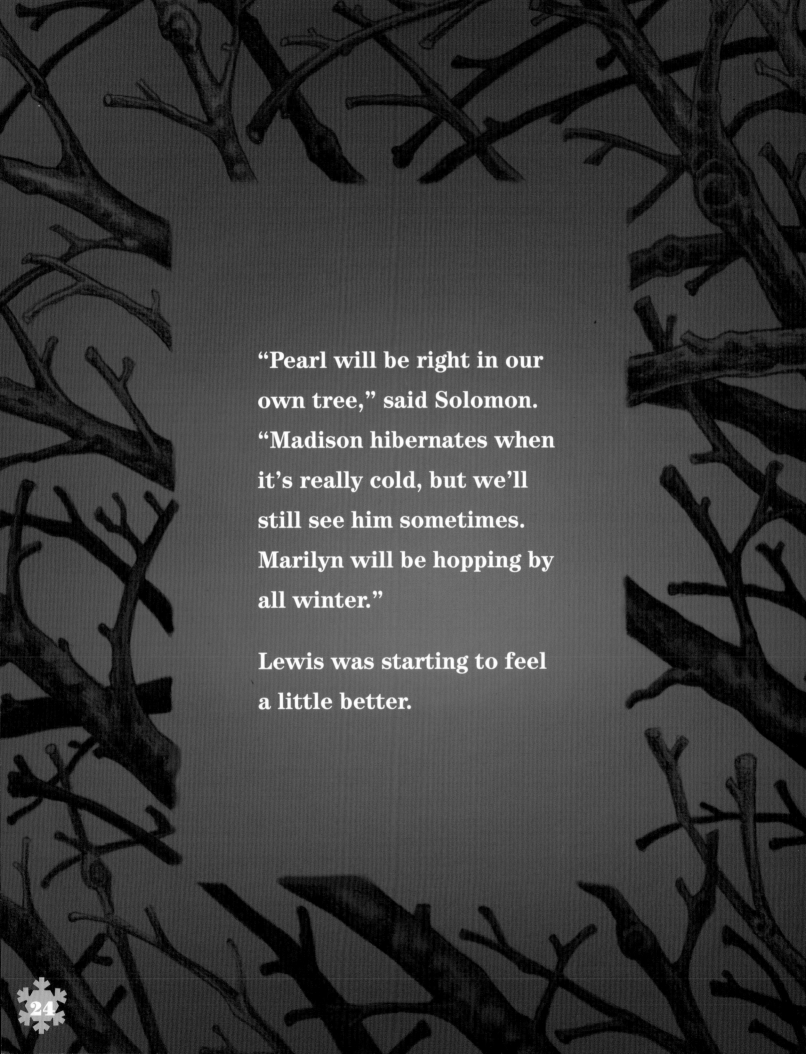

"Pearl will be right in our
own tree," said Solomon.
"Madison hibernates when
it's really cold, but we'll
still see him sometimes.
Marilyn will be hopping by
all winter."

Lewis was starting to feel
a little better.

Then, Solomon pointed to a nearby evergreen tree. There sat a lovely cardinal, singing a sweet song. Lewis darted to the tree and perched beside the pretty bird.

"I'm Cheri Cardinal," the pretty bird warbled. "Are you going to be here all winter, like me?"

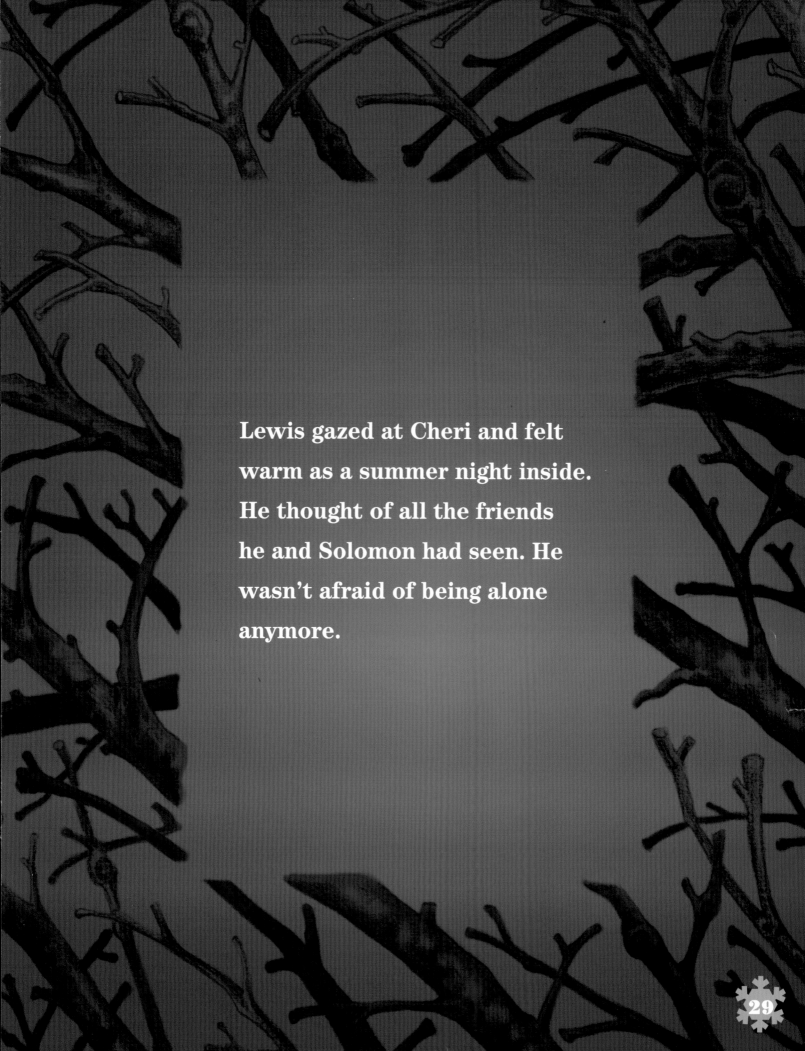

Lewis gazed at Cheri and felt warm as a summer night inside. He thought of all the friends he and Solomon had seen. He wasn't afraid of being alone anymore.

Solomon smiled down on the pair of cardinals, so beautiful in the evergreen tree. He thought, "It's going to be a very good winter after all."